The Amazing SpongeBob

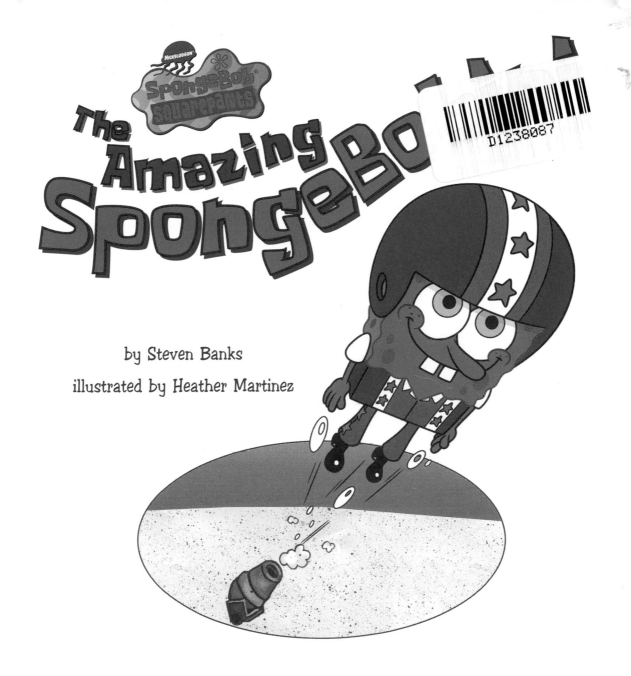

by Steven Banks

illustrated by Heather Martinez

SCHOLASTIC INC.

New York Toronto London Auckland Sydney
Mexico City New Delhi Hong Kong Buenos Aires

Stephen Hillenburg

Based on the TV series *SpongeBob SquarePants*® created by Stephen Hillenburg as seen on Nickelodeon®

ISBN 0-439-53969-2

12 11 10 9 8 7 6 5 4 3 2 1   3 4 5 6 7 8/0

Printed in the U.S.A.

First Scholastic printing, September 2003

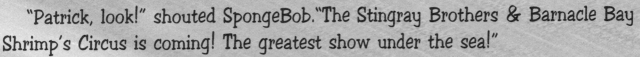

"Patrick, look!" shouted SpongeBob. "The Stingray Brothers & Barnacle Bay Shrimp's Circus is coming! The greatest show under the sea!"

"Too bad we don't live under the sea," said Patrick. "I wish the circus would come to Bikini Bottom."

"Patrick, Bikini Bottom *is* under the sea!" SpongeBob said.

"Oh," said Patrick, scratching his head, "I always wondered why there were so many fish around here."

The next day SpongeBob knocked on Patrick's rock. "Patrick, it's circus time! We'd better leave now so we can get seats by the jugglers and clowns. Real, live clowns, Patrick! Let's go!"

There was no answer. He knocked again. "Patrick?" called SpongeBob.

SpongeBob lifted the rock and saw Patrick lying in bed. "Patrick, what are you doing in bed?" he asked. "We're going to the circus!"

Patrick shook his head sadly. "I can't go to the circus, SpongeBob. I'm sick!"

"Don't worry," said SpongeBob. "I know how to make you feel better. I'll sing you the 'Get Well' song. My grandma used to sing it to me when I was sick."

SpongeBob cleared his throat and began to sing:

"Get well, Patrick. Don't be sick!
This little song will do the trick!
La, la, la—you'll feel better,
by the time I knit this sweater!"

The song didn't work. Patrick was still sick.
"I know—I'll do the 'Get Well' dance!" said SpongeBob.
He began to jump around Patrick's bed. But that didn't work either.

Next SpongeBob tried hypnotizing Patrick.
"Look deep into my eyes and listen to my soothing voice. You are not sick, Patrick. You will go to the circus with your best friend, SpongeBob."

"AH-CHOO!" Patrick sneezed.

SpongeBob patted Pat's head, "Well, we gave it the old boating-school try. . . . See you later, Patrick. I'm off to the most fabulous, amazing, colossal circus ever!"

Patrick grabbed SpongeBob. "But you've got to stay here!" he pleaded. "You have to get sick too! Then we can be sick together and miss the circus together and not have any fun together!"

"Uh, that sounds great, Patrick," said SpongeBob. "But I'm not sick and I really, really, really want to see the circus!"

"Fine!" said Patrick. "Go! I'll just be sick and miss the circus and not have fun all by myself!"

"Great! I knew you'd understand," SpongeBob called over his shoulder. "I'll bring you some of those circus peanuts you love so much!"

SpongeBob gazed up at the huge, red circus tent. "So *that's* why they call it the big top," he said as he handed over his ticket.

SpongeBob hurried to his seat right next to the ring. "Ladies and gentlemen!" called the ringmaster. "Welcome to the greatest show under the sea!"

It *was* the greatest show under the sea. There were acrobats and jugglers, trapeze artists and tightrope walkers, and they even shot a fish out of a cannon! SpongeBob was eating popcorn and watching the show.

"Wow!" cried SpongeBob, "Isn't this the greatest show you've ever seen, Patrick?" He turned and looked at the empty seat beside him. SpongeBob had forgotten that Patrick wasn't there.

Everyone was laughing at the clowns except for SpongeBob. He couldn't stop thinking about Patrick. He started to cry. "I can't enjoy the circus while my best friend is home sick! Patrick needs me. I must return to his bedside and do what any self-respecting sponge would do for a friend in need!"

Patrick was asleep in bed when suddenly he heard a voice outside that woke him up.

"Ladies and gentlemen and all starfish named Patrick!" yelled the voice.

My name is Patrick, thought Patrick. And I'm a starfish!

He got out of bed and lifted up his rock and he couldn't believe what he saw. . . .

SpongeBob was wearing a top hat and a fake mustache. "Welcome to the second greatest show under the sea, SpongeBob's Almost-as-Good-as-a-Real-Circus Circus!" he announced.

Patrick jumped up and down excitedly. "Where is the circus? Where is it? Where?"

"It's *me!*" said SpongeBob. "*I'm* the circus!"

Patrick looked puzzled. "But you don't look like a circus. You look like SpongeBob."

"Just watch!" said SpongeBob.

"Our first act will be SpongeBobini the amazing juggler!" said SpongeBob. "I will attempt to balance ten Krabby Patties on my head while juggling five spatulas!"

"And now prepare yourselves for the death-defying tightrope walk of terror!" he continued.

Patrick hid under his pillow. "That sounds scary! Tell me when it's over! I can't look!"

"And now the Amazing SpongeBobini will swallow a clarinet!" said SpongeBob. "Don't try this at home, kids!"

"Too late," mumbled Patrick.

SpongeBob performed all the different acts he had seen at the circus.

"And now for the grand finale—a brave, handsome soul will be shot out of a cannon!" announced SpongeBob.

"Be careful brave, handsome soul!" shouted Patrick.

SpongeBob took a final bow, exhausted.

Patrick clapped and cheered. "That was a great circus, SpongeBob! I wish you could have been there to see it! Now you sit down and I'll show you what you missed."

SpongeBob smiled. "Wait a minute. Aren't you sick?" he asked.

"Not anymore!" shouted Patrick. "The circus cured me!"